BORN LUCKY
AND OTHER TALES OF THE PAST

Compiled by Tony Bradman

D1434351

Stories by
Geraldine McCaughrean, Jean Ure
and Jacqueline Wilson

Illustrations by Gary Andrews,
Neil Chapman and Douglas Carrel

Contents

Born Lucky

Written by
Geraldine McCaughrean

Illustrated by Gary Andrews

Some babies are just born ugly. It's not their fault. It's not anyone's fault. It doesn't mean they grow up to be ugly. It doesn't mean they grow up stupid or unpleasant. It's just the way they look. It's just their bad luck.

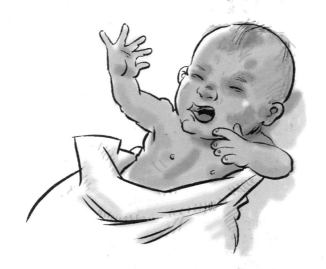

On the face of it, Davus' sister was the unluckiest baby of all. She was yellow and blotchy, with puffy eyes and a smear of hair. When her mother laid her, newborn, at her husband's feet, he looked down and made a face.

'Too ugly,' he said. 'And a girl is no use to me. Put it out.'

Put it out. Like a cat or a puppy.
Put it out. Like a trapped bird or a wasp.
Put it out. Like a candle.

Hoping for a change of heart, Claudia Pulcher searched her husband's face. Now there was *real* ugliness! His cheeks were pitted like old marble and his ears bulged with red hair. His flattened nose was purple from too much wine. And unlike the baby at his feet, Brigonius was ugly both inside and out. He was a bullying husband and an unkind father. His neighbours feared him. His slaves ran away. His horses lay down and died – but not until they had won his races for him: they would not have dared.

Right now, his ugly face was a mask. Right now his poached-egg eyes stared blankly out of the window. He was already thinking again about the Big Race.

His wife did not dare question his decision. She picked up the baby, stiff and quilted in the swaddling clothes, and carried her out of the room.

'On second thoughts …' called Brigonius over his shoulder. His wife turned quickly. '… put it under the new stable. It may bring the horses luck.' Blood could do that: bring luck, or so some people said.

Luck was important to Brigonius. He was a very superstitious man. 'Born-Lucky-Brig' they called him.

Davus saw his mother's face as she left the room. He wanted to help. He wanted to run at his father and kick him in the shins and say, 'Accept my sister! I want a sister!' But he was twelve years old – nearly, and not quite a man. Besides, nobody could kick Brigonius in the shins and live.

Instead, Davus went with his mother to the site of the new stable. As yet, it was no more than a square of ditches, awaiting the brick foundations. Brigonius was building it with prize money from his racing.

'I cannot do it,' said Claudia. She did not cry: a good Roman mother never cried in front of her son. She simply said, 'I cannot do it, Davus. Do it for me.' Then, handing him the baby, she ran back to the house.

Davus looked down at his unwanted, unlovely sister. She had no name. Girls only got a name on the eighth day of life, and then only if they were to be kept.

She opened and shut her mouth like a fish. Her milky blue eyes looked in two directions at once.

'I'm Davus,' he told the baby. 'You chose the wrong day to be born. The 24th of August is unlucky. The gates of the Underworld are open today. Ships sink. Enemies attack. People die.' The baby yawned. 'Tomorrow I become a man, you know? Father is taking me to the barbers for my first shave! How about that?' The baby raised a fist that brushed his beardless cheek. 'I know, I know, but there is *some*. Here, see?' He lifted his chin to show the few soft wisps growing there. In showing it, his fingers touched the charm around his neck: his bulla.

He had worn it ever since his ninth day of life. Tomorrow that would go too, along with his 'beard'.

Davus set the baby down in one of the ditches and walked away. But he could still hear her soft snuffling. Suddenly, for no thought-out reason, he ran back. He did not *want* his father's new stable to be lucky. He did not *want* his father's horses to win. Not if this was what it took to be lucky.

Picking up the baby, Davus began to run – out of the courtyard, along the road. He ran and ran, his sandals slapping the smooth stones of the roadway. He ran past the garrison and into town, until he came to a house with gardens and hives and a chicken shed.

The chickens in the yard grew very excited when Davus climbed over the wall. 'Shhhhh!' he told them. But they jumped and fluttered around him, making enough noise to call out an army. Every moment he expected a slave to spot him and shout, 'Stop! Thief!'

Seeing a tub of grain, Davus grabbed up large handfuls and threw them on the ground. The hens were instantly quiet, pecking up the seeds of their extra meal. Then Davus crept inside the chicken coop, found a soft, hidden place for the baby and laid her down. Let the *hens* be lucky. Let their *eggs* be lucky, but not Born-Lucky-Brig! he thought.

Davus pulled the bulla from around his neck and tied it round the baby's neck instead. 'Here. You have it. I won't need it after tomorrow,' he said. 'A lucky charm for an unlucky baby.'

Davus was just creeping away when the ruler of the roost came strutting back – a big, black, angry-looking cockerel with a slicing black beak. The idea of that beak jabbing the baby's soft little face was so horrible that, before he knew it, Davus had picked up the cockerel, put it under his arm and clambered back over the wall. 'She's ugly enough already, without your help,' he told the outraged, struggling bird.

He had not meant to steal it, but somehow there it was an hour later – gobbling and pecking about among his mother's chickens: a big black brute, bullying the chickens as Brigonius bullied his chicken-hearted family.

By next day, Brigonius could think only of the Big Race, when he would compete in front of Caesar himself! Brigonius was the Town Governor's favoured charioteer. He had started out as a soldier, of course, but his skill with horse and chariot had released him from a soldier's duties and freed him to race on behalf of the Governor. His good luck had made him richer and more famous than some war heroes.

The Governor called him lucky because he drove like a demon and always won. The soldiers at the barracks called him lucky because he no longer had to go on route marches or drill with weapons and a full pack. They called him lucky because he was allowed to keep a wife and son, and even had a villa of his own.

But Brigonius left nothing to luck. As he said all too often: a wise man makes his own luck. He kept birds-of-good-omen in a cage in the garden, so he was sure to see one every day. He wore lucky charms, studied his horoscope and, on special occasions like this, even visited an augur.

Today was his son's birthday, his coming-of-age, his first shave. But though Brigonius took his son into town, he was thinking only of the Big Race that afternoon. He had more important things to do before they visited the barber, he said. And to Davus' horror, Brigonius turned off the road at the house with gardens and hives and a chicken shed.

This is the house! Davus thought to himself in a panic. *This is where I left her! He must know what I did! Someone must have seen me!*

A slave opened the gate. 'Tell your master that Brigonius the Charioteer is here,' said Brigonius.

A man in a saffron robe came shuffling out, smiling and nodding. So this was the house of the augur! Davus had only gone and dumped the baby at the house of the local fortune-teller!

'I race in front of Caesar today!' boasted Brigonius. 'Ask your birds how the day will go for me … Has Africanus called here yet?'

'Not yet, but he always buys a sacrificial bird here, so he will be along later. Shall I give him your greetings?'

'You can give him the plague for all I care,' snarled Brigonius.

They walked into the yard, where the chickens were still strutting about as they had the day before. Davus was convinced that at any moment, the baby hidden in the chicken coop would cry out and be found! His father would recognise that puffy yellow face, those squinty eyes. Davus would be lucky if he lived long enough to see the barber's razor …

The augur passed Brigonius a plate of grain and Brigonius threw some of it in among the chickens. They boggled at him with yellow eyes, but they did not eat. Furious, Brigonius threw another handful at the birds. They drew in their heads and ran away. Charioteer, boy and fortune-teller waited for them to come back and eat. And all the while Davus' eyes rested on the chicken coop where his baby sister lay hidden.

Please, please EAT before they find her!

The words shouted inside his head, over and over.

But, of course, after their extra meal the evening before, the chickens were not that hungry.

The augur sucked his teeth. 'Oh dear. Oh dear, oh dear. The omens are not good, friend. You really should not race today.'

Brigonius gave a great roar of anger, and kicked a chicken into the air. He knew very well that he had to race whenever the Governor told him to. But never before had the omens been unlucky for Born-Lucky-Brig.

He could barely speak for rage by the time they left. Two chickens dangled from his fist, for sacrifice at the temples of Apollo and Neptune. It was all he could think of to get back his good luck. Remembering why he had brought his son to town, he snatched at Davus' face with a rough, hard hand. 'No beard, look! What d'you mean by it? Lazy mongrel. You haven't been trying, have you!'

Later, inside the barber's shop, Brigonius was still fuming and snorting so loudly that the barber grew nervous. And a nervous barber is the last person a boy wants for his first shave. He scraped the soft skin of Davus' neck and face with a trembling blade, then began to hack at his hair.

'Stop!' cried Brigonius, making the razor jump. 'Where is your bulla?' and he made a grab at his son's neck. The razor slipped and cut deep into the

charioteer's hand, but he barely noticed.
'Your charm! Where is it?'

'I – I – lost it,' mumbled Davus.
'At the bathhouse, I think. I don't know.'
'But you are supposed to give it up
today! How can you give it up if it's lost?
That was my bulla when I was a child!
My own mother gave it me the day I was
named! And you *lost* it?' Davus froze with
terror. Yet his father seemed more

frightened than angry. 'That's the third bad omen! A useless girl-child, the augur's chickens, and now a lost bulla.' He sucked at his cut hand.

'And a cut hand,' said Davus unhelpfully.

Brigonius pulled him out of the barber's chair and into the street, hair half cut. The other customers looked round from their gossiping. Davus wished he could shrink to the size of an ant and crawl away.

Just across the street, Davus' schoolteacher and classmates were doing their lessons under the awning of the bread shop. Naturally, the teacher wanted to know why Davus was not at his lessons. Brigonius answered for him. 'No more school. He's done with all that rubbish. Today my son becomes a man. Today he stops wasting my money and gets down to work.' The schoolboys turned and stared at Davus – at his half-shorn hair. 'I never went to school and look at me! I'm a celebrity – a rich man, me!'

Davus wished he could sink to the pavement, blend in among the other boys, become invisible. History, mathematics and philosophy were suddenly his favourite pastimes.

The Greek schoolmaster dipped his head graciously. 'You are putting him into the army?'

Sweat broke out on Davus' hands. *Oh Zeus, not the army!* His father had once draped armour over him and he had not even been able to stand up under the weight of it!

'No. He can be my groom – maintain the chariot, exercise the horses, polish my armour.'

The teacher narrowed his Greek eyes and looked Brigonius over. 'Slaves can do these things. Davus is very good at his grammar.'

'*Grammar?* What use is *grammar*? No one ever learned me *grammar* and look at me! All teachers are fools. I'll train him up into a charioteer like me. He'll earn more money than you can even count!'

Once again the master dipped his head politely. The other boys looked at Davus enviously. They did not envy him his haircut or his father, but his lucky escape from lessons and his life as a charioteer.

'I didn't know you wanted me to race, Father.' He tried to sound pleased but his voice came out sounding more horrified than glad.

'In time, maybe,' said Brigonius. 'First you have to make yourself useful.'

At last they reached the stadium. Brigonius led Davus down into the under-darkness, where the horses stood tethered to one wall, the chariots lined up along the other. Davus fetched his father's two milk-white mares – but Brigonius did the harnessing himself. Suddenly, his voice dropped to an urgent whisper. 'Good. We are here ahead of Africanus. This is his chariot – this silvered one alongside mine. When I've gone, sneak under and take out the link pin.'

'Do what?'

'Take out the pin! Africanus is the only one with a chance of beating me today ... Well? What are you waiting for? Do it. And *don't get seen*.'

Davus gaped at his father.

'Do I have to do it myself?' hissed Brigonius.

'No! No!' said Davus.

Misunderstanding, his father patted Davus' half-cut hair. 'Good boy. How often have I told you: a man has to make his own luck.' Then he was gone – to put on his red kid tunic with its fillets of bronze and leather, his moulded breastplate and splendid helmet with its crest of dyed horsehair.

Twelve chariots stood in the shadowy chariot-room – a wall of beaten bronze, their wheel-blades overlapping. Here and there, slaves stood polishing metal or grooming horses.

Davus ducked under his father's
chariot and began to worm his way
across to the one next to it. He did not
want to, but he dared not fail his father.

In the dark, his fingers instantly
came down on something – a hand?
An ankle?

'Ow!'

At first he could not see the other
groom because of the darkness. Then he
made out the glimmer of eyes and teeth.

'Hail, friend. Just checking the lashings,' said the teeth.

'Hail, friend. Me too,' replied Davus.

'I'm Tertius, son of Flavius Africanus. I haven't seen you before.'

'Davus. Son of Brigonius,' said Davus.

'Ah! The great Born-Lucky-Brig! Not so lucky today, though!'

'How's that?'

'All the luck is with my father today!' Tertius seemed to be nursing some secret he was bursting to tell. 'You'll never guess what happened this morning! My father went to the augur's house to buy a cockerel.'

Davus gulped. 'The augur?'

'Yes. The augur on the Via Nova, know him? We buy a cockerel there every race day – to sacrifice at the temple. But it has to be black. Father will only take black. So the augur went off to find the one he had set by. And do you know what? The cockerel was gone, but he found – you'll never believe it!' (Davus knew that he would.) 'He found a *baby*!'

'A ...'

'The augur says that an eagle must have dropped it and carried off the bird instead! He was dancing about, pointing at the sky, shouting, "Such an omen! Such a happy omen!" *So* funny!' (Even Davus could not help smiling.) 'Of course he may have put it there himself – to attract business, you know? Babies don't usually drop out of the sky. But Father is happy and he always races better when he thinks luck is on his side.'

Davus said nothing. What could he say? Then a dreadful thought struck him. 'He didn't sacrifice the baby, did he? Instead of the cockerel?'

'What do you take us for? No! He's going to adopt her, of course! So I've got a new sister! A bit startling: a white baby in an Ethiope family, but Father is a great one for good luck. Anyway, he says all children are a gift from the gods.'

'Even girls?' said Davus, marvelling.

Tertius looked at him oddly. 'Of course girls. Father says you Romans don't have nearly enough children.'

Above them, the stands were filling with people. A cheer went up as the Governor arrived with his guest who took place of honour. Down in the chariot-room, Davus said, 'I'm sure your father will win. A baby dropped by an eagle must be a very lucky omen. You should call her Fortunata.'

'Or Victoria, if Father wins.'

'I'd like to see her, this amazing baby.'

'Come any time,' said Tertius.

Into the room came the huge, black
Flavius Africanus, alongside the huger
Brigonius whose purple nose shone like
a plum. Shoulder-to-shoulder they
strode to their chariots, stepping up on

to the baseboards. The blades on their wheels clashed as their sons led the horses out.

Soon, all the chariots rolled out into the bright sunlight of the arena. Cheers and stamping greeted them. The Governor leaned over to Caesar and pointed out Brigonius.

Side by side, Davus and Tertius stood in the tunnel entrance. 'I'm glad I checked the link pin,' said Tertius. 'You wouldn't believe how often the grooms try to sabotage each other's chariots.' And he gave Davus a quick, odd, sideways look.

'I'm glad you checked the link pin, too,' said Davus, and meant it with all his heart. *Father will just have to make his own luck today, won't he?* he thought. Then he started to laugh. It was the first time he had laughed for days.

'You must come and see our new baby,' said Tertius.

'And you must come and see our new black cockerel,' said Davus and laughed harder than ever.

The charioteers saluted Caesar.
They wore their reins wound round their
chests and their helmets gleamed
in the sun. Vain and glamorous, they
circled the stadium while the crowds
cheered and stamped. Then they lined
up for the start. At the drop of a flag
they were away.

On his cushioned seat, under a purple silk canopy, the Governor turned to Caesar and continued his story of the augur's henhouse and the baby dropped by an eagle – the extraordinary omen of good luck. Caesar did not take his eyes from the race but he must have been listening, because when the Governor had finished, he turned and spoke to one of his Imperial Guards.

A minute later, the soldier stood in front of Tertius. 'Where is the eagle-baby?' he demanded. 'Caesar wants to see it.'

'In the arena, Sir! With my mother, Sir!'

'Well, fetch it, boy. Quickly!'

The guard turned on his heel. Tertius bit his lip. 'Now he will adopt her himself. I just know it!' he said. 'Caesar will want all that good luck!'

Davus tried to imagine it. His sister, adopted by an emperor. But no. There was such a thing as *too much* good luck. He watched Tertius run, climbing and circling the steep seating of the amphitheatre to find his mother and the marvellous 'eagle-baby'.

Meanwhile, the chariots hurtled around the track, sometimes clashing wheels, sometimes hitting the barriers. One overturned. Brigonius went swiftly into the lead, with Africanus close behind – so close that Brigonius was able to strike the black horses with the stock of his whip. All the while, he kept up a stream of curses – cursing his horses, his rivals, the track, the augur, the cut on his hand, the missing bulla, those chickens … His bad luck chewed on him. But a grin returned as his lead increased.

Tertius was coming back now with the baby, carrying it to show Caesar. A bodyguard stopped him, wanting to know his business. Tertius held up the baby.

Out of the corner of his eye, Brigonius saw the baby held aloft. Even at such a distance, even driving at breakneck speed through flying sand, he recognised it. Something about the swaddling – the smear of hair on the

yellow head. The sight struck him in the
eye like an arrow.

His concentration broke. He turned
to look again, and the reins round his
body steered the horses left. A wheel
clipped the barrier. The trace pin
sheared through. The front of the
chariot sagged and Brigonius went over
the top of it. Bound to the horses by the
reins, he was dragged not once but twice
around the stadium, the mares so
scared of him that
they dared not
stop.

As Africanus overtook, his sandy dust coated the white horses in red dirt. Africanus had won!

Under the purple canopy, Caesar turned and regarded the baby in Tertius' arms. 'What an unfortunate-looking child!' he exclaimed. 'I was going to adopt it, but, *blurgh*! Take it away!'

The Greek doctor on duty at the stadium prescribed powdered horn for baby Victoria's yellow jaundice. Within days, it was cured. She was as pink and bonny as the best of babies.

As treatment for countless cuts and bruises, the doctor had Brigonius smothered daily, from head to foot, in fresh goat dung.

The Valley
of the Crocuses

Written by
Jean Ure

Illustrated by Neil Chapman

Crogdene – the valley of the crocuses. Spring was here, and the land a mass of yellow flowers all the way down to the banks of the river.

Caroc and his new hound puppy were playing in the sunshine. His father had given him the puppy. Thrown it at him.

'If you want it so badly, then have it!'

The puppy was one of a litter of three produced by Brenna, his father's favourite hunting dog. It had been a disappointing litter. Two of the pups had died at birth, the third had been born lame. It had a crippled front paw that twisted inwards. Cered, Caroc's father, had been going to drown it. What use was a crippled dog? But Caroc had begged for its life to be spared. It was such a little thing! All squirming and helpless.

Caroc knew what it was like to be squirming and helpless. He knew what it was like not to be wanted. He and his pup were two of a kind, for Caroc had a withered hand and would never be able to join the hunt with his brothers. Sometimes the other boys jeered at him and once they had lain in wait and jumped on him. Caroc had fought. Oh, he had fought! He was not his father's son for nothing. But the other boys were bigger and stronger, and who would have cared if they had done him serious harm? He was of no more use than Brenna's pup with its twisted paw.

It was his sister Fion who had come to his rescue. She had rushed in, shouting, and driven the boys off with a stick. Perhaps Fion would care if they had injured him. But she was the only one.

Fion had spoken up for Caroc when he begged his father for the puppy.

'May he not have it, Father? It would mean so much to him!'

That was when Cered had contemptuously tossed it to him across the floor of the hut.

'Just keep it out of my way,' he'd growled.

The pup was four months old now. Caroc called her Brave Heart, which made Fion laugh and shake her head.

'She will have need of a brave heart if she is to survive.'

'She will survive,' said Caroc. 'She has me to look after her!'

'Then of course she will live to grow old and wise,' agreed Fion. Secretly she thought that Caroc, too, would have need of a strong heart. Life would not be easy for either of them.

The pup had Brenna's coat, grey and shaggy, like most of the hounds in the village, but none of Brenna's long-legged grace and ease of movement. But to Caroc she was beautiful. He and his Brave Heart went everywhere together. At night they slept in each other's arms. By day they roved the valley, but always keeping an eye on his father's hut down in the village.

Caroc's mother, Eridwen, had warned him:

'Do not venture too far. The times are troubled. Stay close to home.'

There had been talk, in the huts at night, of Saxon hordes ravaging the countryside. The Romans, who had been in the land for as long as anyone could remember, from way back before time, were no longer as powerful as once they had been. Rumour had it that they were preparing to pull out, to sail back across the sea to the place called Rome where they had come from all those centuries ago.

Caroc knew nothing of Rome and

very little more of the Romans. He knew that they had constructed great towns, and roads running straight as arrows leading to far-off places, but they were of no importance to him in his daily life.

He had seen Romans, of course. Everyone had seen them, for they came to the village. Caroc had even seen the legions, marching. A sight to stir the blood! But no Roman had ever spoken to him, nor did he ever expect to travel their roads or see their towns. What were Romans to him?

'They keep us safe,' muttered Fion.

The Romans, with their chariots and their shining helmets ... arrogantly striding the land, raising taxes, in control. It was hard to imagine life without them. Warlike tribes might rejoice at the thought of their downfall, but there was fear in the hearts of the villagers.

The young boys boasted of what they would do if the painted hordes should come. One of Caroc's brothers, Corwen, declared he would stand his ground and fight them off with dagger and spear. The way he spoke, he made it sound as if he would tackle the whole horde single-handed.

Fion said that she would sooner die than be taken prisoner. They had all heard what the Painted People did with the women they captured.

'You will not be captured!' said Corwen. 'I shall defend you.'

But Fion shook her head. She was a year older than Corwen, and she knew better. If the hordes came, there would be no defence.

'I will fight!' said Caroc; but Corwen curled his lip and Fion laughed.

'You are too young!'

'He is too crippled,' said Corwen.

'He is too young!' Fion turned on him savagely. She had a temper, did Fion. 'Nine years old! He will do no fighting.'

'Maybe they won't come,' said Caroc.

But plans were made, just in case. The hills all around were densely wooded; the entire village could hide in those hills and not be found. The women urged that they should all go – men and women alike, with the children. A handful of farmers would stand no chance against the Saxon hordes.

But some of the men were for staying put; Caroc's father and brothers amongst them. Death, declared Corwen, however bloody, was better than fleeing like a whipped cur.

'Stupid,' muttered Fion, but what did she know? A mere girl!

Deep pits were dug where workmen could bury their precious tools, in the hope of recovering them at a later date. And Caroc was told repeatedly, 'not to venture too far'.

He was playing with Brave Heart on the bank of the river then he saw Fion come running towards him, waving her arms and shouting.

'Caroc, Caroc! Come quickly!'

Caroc scrabbled his way back up the bank, followed by the pup.

'What is it?'

'Quick! It is time!' She caught him by the hand. 'We must go!'

She made to rush him off, but Caroc snatched his hand away from her and scooped Brave Heart into his arms. He wasn't leaving his dog.

'Hurry, hurry!' Fion grabbed his sleeve, hustling him along.

'Put that animal down!' roared Caroc's mother, when she saw him.

'No!' Caroc hugged the pup protectively. With her twisted paw, she would never be able to keep up.

Eridwen hunched her shoulders. 'As you please!' If the boy wished to lag behind and die, then let him. She had more important things to worry about. Eridwen was with child. And this time, may it please the gods, she would give birth to an infant sound in wind and limb; not another cripple.

Caroc ran, as best he could, with Brave Heart in his arms. They had to cross the river and reach the safety of the hills. It was not easy, running across the rough ground and all the time hugging the pup with his one good hand. But she was his dog and he would not abandon her.

Even as they reached the ford, where the water was shallow enough for them to wade across, they could hear the harsh sounds of the Saxon war cries, the terrified lowing of cattle and the clashing of weapons.

'Caroc!' screamed Fion.

She was halfway across the river when she realised he was not with them. He was struggling along behind, with the dog still in his arms.

'*Caroc!*' She turned, and waded back.
'Put her down! Leave her!'

'No!'

Caroc fought, but Fion was too strong.
She tore the pup from his grasp and
hurled her to the ground, then seized
Caroc by the arm and dragged him into
the water. Gasping, he had no choice but
to stumble after her. The water came up
to his knees – up to his waist – up to his
shoulders. But at last he was across. He
had just the time for one quick look back.
The pup was on the river bank,
whimpering in fear and bewilderment.

Her master had gone and she was left
behind! A sob rose in Caroc's throat.
What would become of her?

'Come!' Fion was at his side, urging
him on. 'It cannot be helped. She must
fend for herself.'

But she was too young, and too little.
With her twisted paw she would never be
able to swim across the river!

'Caroc, this is no time to be thinking
of a mere dog.'

Fion took him by his good hand and
jerked him roughly forward. 'If you are
to survive, you must think of yourself.'

For days and nights – how many, Caroc was unable to tell – they hid in the forest, drinking from streams, eating what they could find or catch. Some of the dogs had come with them and brought down the odd rabbit or squirrel. They managed to stay alive, but their hearts were heavy.

Great leaping flames rose from the valley. By night a red glow could be seen. Caroc knew that it was the village, burning. He knew that the Painted People would have carried off whatever was of value to them, then torched what was left. Probably butchered all the livestock. Set fire to the fields. Killed his father, killed his brothers. But what of Brave Heart?

The thought tormented him. His father had reckoned Caroc a thing of no worth; his brothers, at best, had ignored him. But Brave Heart! She had loved him. She had depended on him. And he had let her down.

As soon as it was thought safe to go back, they crept down the hillside to pick up the pieces of their shattered lives. Caroc had but one thought: to find his pup. Could she have survived, amidst all the death and destruction?

She was not where he had last seen her, on the river bank by the ford. He had been nursing a secret hope that perhaps she might have stayed there, waiting for him to come back.

'Brave Heart!' He called her name and stood, listening. 'Brave Heart! Are you there?'

And then he heard it, the sound of whimpering. It was coming from further down the river. He turned, and ran.

'Brave Heart!' he cried. 'Where are you?'

He found her at last. She was caught
in a bed of reeds, tangled up, unable to
move. She must have followed him into
the river, then lost her footing and been
carried downstream. The reeds had
saved her from drowning, but she was
trembling with fear and bone thin.
Caroc could see her ribs, like pieces of
twig.

He had to find a way of rescuing her!
It was of no use asking Fion or any of the
others for help. They were too busy,
picking their way through the devastated
remains of their village. But he knew
that if the pup were not plucked from

the water very soon, she would die.

A short way further on there was a willow tree, its leaves trailing in the river. Caroc rushed to it and clambered up. He edged himself out, along one of the branches. It sank down, dangerously low. Caroc stretched out a hand. Brave Heart cried, piteously. But it was no use. He couldn't reach her.

'Brave Heart! He sobbed. 'Oh, Brave Heart!'

The years moved on. Sixteen centuries came and went. The world entered a new millennium. Crogdene had become Croydon – no longer the valley of the crocuses. Where once the river had flowed, there was thick black tarmac. Where once the crocuses had bloomed there was pavement, grimy and cracked. Buildings stood where the forest had been. Caroc's village, which had grown again, had long since disappeared. A Saxon settlement had sprung up in its place, but that too had gone, centuries and centuries ago, buried beneath the long march of civilisation. Caroc would not have recognised the place where it had stood. Grey concrete covered it, and cars belched fumes into the stale air.

In Old Town, they were pulling down some buildings. A boy called Tom (who for all anyone knew could have been one of Caroc's descendants) had been watching in great excitement from his bedroom window. One day they had come with a bulldozer and crumbled a whole row of houses.

Then they had come with a lorry and removed the rubble. Yesterday they had brought what his dad called 'heavy plant' and dug a simply enormous hole. The most enormous hole that Tom had ever seen. They had put a wooden fence all round to stop people getting in there, but from his window Tom could still see the hole. It was so big and so deep he reckoned you could get about a hundred people in it. Ever since they had started digging, Tom had had but one desire: to get behind that fence and have a closer look …

He knew just how he would do it. He had inspected the fence closely: there was a place where it didn't quite reach the ground. A grown-up could never manage to wriggle through. But a boy could.

There was only one problem: Tom's mum had warned him to keep away from that building site.

'It's dangerous,' she said. 'And it's dirty. I don't want you going there.'

But she didn't actually make him promise.

'Mum,' said Tom, on Sunday morning. 'Can I take Prince out?'

Prince was the family dog, a handsome German Shepherd.

'Yes, if you want,' said Mum. 'Where are you going? To the park?'

Tom made a mumbling sound which could have meant yes or could have meant no. Then he slipped Prince on the lead and went racing over the road before his mum could look out of the front room window and see where he was headed.

The workmen weren't there on a
Sunday morning; the building site was
deserted. First Tom and then Prince
squeezed their way under the fence. Now
they were safe! Mum wouldn't be able to
see them unless she went upstairs and
looked out of Tom's window, and she
wasn't very likely to do that. Not when
she was busy in the kitchen, cooking
Sunday dinner. And Dad was out the
back, digging a hole of his own. A silly
little mimsy hole for planting things in.
Not a patch on Tom's hole.

Tom's hole was … magnificent. A hole amongst holes! Tom stood there, gazing down into it. And as he gazed, he was filled with another desire: a desire to fetch a plank, and place it across one corner of the hole, and walk across it.

'Stay there,' he said to Prince. 'On guard!'

Tom trotted off across the building site. Prince sat down by the side of the hole. He had been told to guard it, and guard it he would, though he couldn't

quite see what there was to guard. It was just a hole. There was nothing in there. At least, nothing that anyone could see …

But something that a dog could hear!

Prince cocked his head to one side. His ears pricked up. Slowly he rose to his feet. His whole body had suddenly stiffened, on the alert.

What was that?

Tom turned, with his plank.

'Oy! Prince!' he bellowed.

But too late. Prince had taken a flying leap into the hole…

In later years, when he was an old, old man hunkered round the fire, Caroc was fond of telling his grandchildren the story of the Saxon horde; how they had sacked his village and murdered his father and brothers. How he and his sister Fion had run off to hide in the woods. How his pup had tried to follow and had had to be left behind.

The part that they loved best, the part they always waited for, was when he told how he had found her again, caught in the reeds and half-dead. How he had edged out on the branch of a willow and risked drowning, but still hadn't been able to reach her.

'How you thought you had lost her,' they prompted.

How he thought he had lost her; but how, all of a sudden, this great dog, like a wolf, had appeared out of nowhere.

'And you were scared!'

'And I was scared,' agreed Caroc. He had feared the wolf was going to take his pup and carry her off.

'But it didn't!'

'No, it didn't.'

Instead, it had picked her up in its mouth and swum with her to the bank, where Caroc had stood, helpless and trembling. It had deposited her – gently! Oh, so gently! – amongst the crocuses, and then disappeared just as suddenly as it had come.

'Like a dream, yet it was no dream.'

'And the pup grew strong!'

'And the pup grew strong,' said
Caroc. 'And she became the very best
dog that a man could have.'

The story of Caroc and his dog went down in history. It was a tale that was told long after he had gone.

And here was the odd thing. When Prince pulled himself up out of the hole, out of that hole that was dry as a bone, he was dripping wet. And in his collar was caught a yellow flower. A crocus...

The Daughter

Written by
Jacqueline Wilson

Illustrated by Douglas Carrel

I turn the handle of the spit. Turn and
turn and turn. The fat from the fowl
splatters my face. The great fire scorches
me until I am half-cooked myself.

I turn and turn and turn though my back is breaking, turn though my hands are blistered. My mouth is so dry I can barely swallow but I finished my mug of small beer an hour ago. I am so weary that my eyes start closing, c-l-o-s-i-n-g ...

'Keep turning, you useless feeble girl!' roars the Master Meat Cook.

The other scullions snigger.

The Cook is kind to the boys. He gives them the choicest left-overs and when they've done their chores he joins them in their games of football in the gardens.

The Cook throws the blown-up pig's bladder at my head, knocking me smartly so that my eyes sting.

'There! That will wake you up,' he says.

He hates me. He hates me even though I am his daughter, his only child. He hates me *because* I am his daughter, his only child. He hates me because I killed my mother.

She was the Sweetmeat Cook. When my father speaks of her, he savours her

name as if her own rosewater candies were melting on his tongue. They were brought up together in the Palace kitchens, childhood sweethearts. They wed whcn they came of age and were delighted when my mother grew big with child. A lusty boy to follow in his father's footsteps at the Palace.

But I was a girl, a red-faced bawling babe who nearly tore my mother apart. She took me in her arms at last and I stared at her with my great green eyes.

'Witch's eyes,' says my father, spitting. 'You looked at your mother and put a curse on her. She died of a fever three days after.'

He's never said it, but I know he wishes I'd died too. But he paid for me to be brought up in the village, and when I was six, he took me to live with him inside the Palace. Not as his child. As the junior scullion. To scrub and scrape and steep – and to turn and turn and turn the spit for the roasting meat. Boar and beef, capons, pheasants, quails and swans.

When Father thwacks the sides of meat with his axe his face is contorted and I jump at each thud. When he skewers each limp bird body I tremble. When he chops off a head I shut my eyes tight.

I have to scurry round and sweep up

the eyes and beaks, the paws and claws, the reeking ribbons of innards. Once I saved two severed swan's wings and tried to work out how to fix them to my back so I could fly far away. The wings withered and started to smell and I had to throw them on the rubbish heap. I tried straddling the kitchen broom but my feet stayed flat on the floor.

My father thinks me a witch but I see no evidence of any magic powers, black or white.

I pretend though. It's the only way I can stop the other scullions making my life even more of a misery. When their pokes and prods become too vicious I raise my head and stare straight at them, widening my eyes until they water.

'Lizzie's giving us the witch's eyes!' they say, giggling nervously. 'Foolish girl! Can't scare us.'

But they back away, ducking their heads, out of my line of sight. I scare them all right.

I once tried the eye trick on Father, when I caught him in the corner with the Pudding Cook, the woman who was once my poor dead mother's friend. I thought of Mother underneath the cold earth, eternally unembraced. I widened my eyes – and Father saw me over her shoulder.

He hit me then. He beat me until neither of my witch's eyes could open and for days, the kitchen was a blur.

Turn and turn and turn. The spit is chock-a-block with flesh and fowl and there's still a vast heap of dead creatures waiting in the wet room. We are preparing for a huge celebratory banquet. The new Queen has withdrawn to her chambers and started her labours at dawn today. We are all awaiting the birth of the little Prince.

In the cool at the far end of the kitchen the Sugar Cook has fashioned a sugar cradle that really rocks, and now he is modelling a marchpane babe, its

head eerily real, its arms and legs neatly tucked up, its bare bottom on show for all to gawp at.

'And if it's a girl they can always pull off its twiddly bit,' one of the scullions giggles.

The Sauce Cook hits him with her ladle and my father frowns. It is not a laughing matter. The King has to have a son and heir. That is why he discarded the first Queen and little Princess. Now he has the new Queen, the one they whisper is also a witch. She has certainly bewitched the King, but so long as she gives birth to a fine healthy son she will need no magic charms.

It will be a son. The finest astrologers in the land have consulted their charts and declared it to the King. The Royal Physicians have prodded the Queen beneath her farthingale and agreed that the unborn infant is definitely a male child. The Queen's Ladies have performed all the usual tests and tricks and each and every time they are united in their testimony: a boy.

The Palace is agog with the good news – but as the hours progress there is a growing tension. The Queen's chambers are at the other end of the Palace, but every now and then I fancy I can hear her high-pitched screams.

I turn and turn and turn, the fire slow and smouldering for the swan and turkey, but banked up to roaring heat to crisp the pork and sear the game birds. As the hours pass the tensions worsen in the kitchen. Every table is covered with cooked meats, glistening gold and ruby red and rich brown – but maybe this is a banquet that will never be touched.

The new Queen has been in labour for too long. The Pudding Cook scurries the corridors and whispers with her friends in the bed chambers. She tells us that they've sent for the local Wise Woman.

'But she's a witch, everyone knows that!' my father gasps.

'A witch to help a witch,' says the Pudding Cook. 'She knows a secret trick of speeding labour.'

The Wise Woman works her magic charms. Just after four the Pudding Cook comes speeding back down the corridors.

'The babe is born! Alive and well – and the Queen too, though exhausted.'

'The King has his son!' my father shouts, punching the air with his fist, and the kitchen rocks with hurrahs.

'No! No, it is a daughter, a girl!' says the Pudding Cook.

There's a sudden appalled silence.

My father stares at me, his old sorrow sharpening his face.

'Turn!' he shouts.

I turn and turn and turn, eyes lowered, because I do not want another beating.

I roast the bird, though the banquet will be a sad affair. The Sweetmeat Cook mutilates his marchpane babe, decides it is too cruel a reminder, and starts to mix a vat of sugar and eggwhite, intent on wrapping the child with edible swaddling.

There's an order from the King! We are all allowed extra ale to drink the health of the Queen and her new child. Doubtless it would have been fine wine if a boy had been born. But the ale is welcome nonetheless, and the kitchen is soon a merry place for all but me. My father allows the scullions their share of ale too, but I am only permitted my usual small beer which fails to flush the cheeks or fuddle the brain.

My father is very flushed, very fuddled. He is fooling with the Pudding Cook. But then word is sent from the Queen's chambers. Her Majesty is reviving and requires a good posset curd to build up her strength.

The Pudding Cook panics and gets to work with a great clattering of pans. She needs to seethe her milk on the fire so she elbows me out of the way. She starts cracking the eggs in her mixture, one after another, beating clumsily. Her face is red with effort, her hair hanging in her eyes. She fails to stir enough, and the fire is too fierce.

'It's curdling!' she wails. 'It's ruined!'

She turns to me. 'It's all your fault!
You put the evil eye on it.'

She strikes at me with her spoon.
I dodge, my arms flailing – and knock
her whole bowl flying across the floor.
She hits me again, knocking me over,
so I roll into the fire, the fire, the
fire …

My hands, my hands! But someone is
soothing them with cool lotion and
wrapping them in soft linen, singing to
me gently all the while. Is it my mother?
Have I died and gone to Heaven?

I open my eyes. I stare at two orbs as green as my own – but this is an old woman with wrinkles deep in her face and silver hair. She smiles at me, and I smile back in spite of the pain.

'Your daughter will recover,' she says over her shoulder.

'Thank you for your help, Wise Woman,' the Pudding Cook mumbles, chastened.

'I doubt her hands will heal though. She'll be good for nothing if she cannot turn the spit,' says my father. 'What use will the girl be then?'

'Pray let me take your daughter, Master Cook. I will give you a good price for her.'

She tips out half the purse of gold given to her by the Queen. My father does not argue. He stoops and gathers the coins before she can change her mind.

'You gave that vast sum for *me!*' I whisper, stunned, as she leads me away from the Palace on her old mare.

'Your father certainly does not hold you dear!'

'It is because I am evil. I killed my mother.' I confess. 'My father said that I stared at her with my green witch's eyes the day I was born and put a curse on her.'

'What nonsense,' says the Wise Woman, tucking her own shawl about my shoulders. 'All newborn babes have *blue* eyes. I of all women should know that.'

I can scarcely absorb this information.

'Even so,' I whisper, 'why should you waste a fortune on a useless girl-child?'

'Girls are of great value,' says the Wise Woman. 'We are entering a new age. The little red-haired babe born today will make a fine Queen of England.'

She wraps the shawl tight, like mock swaddling. 'And you shall be *my* babe, my little witch daughter – and one day you will be as wise a woman as me.'